Bruised, Not Broken

LaShanna Taylor Sweeney

authorHOUSE®

AuthorHouse™
1663 Liberty Drive
Bloomington, IN 47403
www.authorhouse.com
Phone: 1 (800) 839-8640

Published by AuthorHouse 10/11/2018

ISBN: 978-1-5462-6347-0 (sc)
ISBN: 978-1-5462-6346-3 (e)

Print information available on the last page.

This book is printed on acid-free paper.

Foreword

The author is a trusted friend, a mother, a wife and a mentor.

Anyone who has ever been in a relationship will appreciate reading about the ups and downs of Kaandra and Kevin's relationship and its final outcome. As one reads this book, they'll share in the laughter, the sadness, the frustration, the heart ache and the victory of Kaandra. Kaandra faced many challenges and struggles but through it all, she came out victorious. She refused to keep a victim mentality.

The situations that Kaandra encountered may not be your specific situations. You may not have been any of the people listed in this book and you may not have lived Kaandra's realities, but I'm sure you'll identify with them: difficult and dreadful decisions. There will be something mentioned in this book that every reader will be able to relate to.

Bruised, not broken is a book that gives hope. This book is an easy read as well as inspirational. I recommend this book.

The main thing I recommend: Please! Please! Get to know the entire family of the person you choose to be in a relationship with. I'm expecting readers to be pleased with this book and with the author. This won't be a book that is easily forgotten.

Letitia Nolan

Deep

How can I get you out from within me so deep?

It's only been a week…

My heart and soul weep for you

Even as I sleep

Now, I'm left wonder…

How can I get you, out from within me so deep?

Author LaShanna Taylor Sweeney

*Dedicated to all those who have gone thru a breakup
and didn't know how they were going to get thru it.*

Bruised, Not Broken

Kaandra stared at her phone in a mixture of anticipation and nervousness. She couldn't believe she had done it. She was ready to put the memory of the last year behind her and start anew. Her last year had been filled with panic attacks, counseling, and doctors appointments. A year of fear and nervous breakdowns had been overcome with a simple "okay."

On the internet, she hadn't had to face anyone. She had been anonymous, mostly, just another girl among many. This anonymity and a leave of absence from work led to lots of time to sit and surf the net, which had led her to the Vibrant People Meet website. She'd connected with a lot of interesting people, all while hiding behind her computer monitor.

To cope with her life, Kaandra had started writing a lot of poetry, mostly heartfelt poems that mourned the relationship she'd lost and looked forward hopefully towards more rewarding days and love. That's how Mr. Right had found her. Kevin Right had replied to all of her verses with sincerity and kindness, asking her to delve deeper into their meaning and share with him. Before long, they were conversing online on a daily basis, and after a few months, they arranged their first phone call. He was just like she'd imagined on the phone: kind, smart, and thoughtful with a smooth, deep voice that calmed and excited her all at once. Nothing like her past partners. And she, with the swagger that comes with anonymity, had been able to be an equal conversationalist. She'd been witty, intelligent, and flirtatious at all the right moments.

But today, something had changed. Before hanging up, Mr. Right said quietly, "We've had so many amazing conversations. I would love to meet you—in person."

Kaandra was sure he could hear her intake of breath at his words or the nervous thumping of her heart. She held her breath for what she was sure was an awkwardly long moment for him, before exhaling and saying at once, "Okay, we can meet."

There was a bit more small talk as they arranged the best weekend to meet and ended their call with the normal pleasantries. When Kaandra hung up, she was immediately overwhelmed with excitement and nervousness. She had taken her leap of faith in just three months, but now her thoughts raced and her stomach plummeted. What should she wear? How should she do her hair? What would Kevin actually be like in person? What if he wasn't "Mr. Right"? What if he was? What if it was too soon?

Kaandra paused and placed a hand over her heart to steady herself. One thing at a time. It was just a date. That was all.

Then she turned to her closet to pick out the perfect outfit for taking a leap.

"What if I don't like him, Tara?" Kaandra asked, clinging to her phone. "What if he doesn't like me?"

"It's a bit late for that, isn't it?" her sister Tara said jokingly on the other end of the line. "Calm down. It is just a date. I know it has been a while, but you've been on dates before. Dates are meant to be fun. They don't all have to be set up to find Mr. Right. Just go have fun. You deserve it."

Kaandra knew she was right and told her sister as much. After hanging up, she took a deep breath and began to get ready for her date with Kevin. If she didn't hurry, she was going to be late.

As it turned out, Kaandra got to the mall a little early, which suited her just fine. She'd be able to see Kevin before he saw her. Minutes passed, and then more time passed. Finally, an hour passed and still no sign of him. *I knew he was too good to be true*, Kaandra thought. Defeated, she grabbed her purse and started to head out. As she was opening the door, her phone rang. It was Kevin.

"I'm so sorry," he said. "I got lost on my way. I hope you still want to meet."

Kaandra smiled, but tried her best to hide the disappointment in her tone. "We can meet some other time."

"I'm only a few minutes away. I really would love to see you, even if only for a few minutes."

Kaandra felt the ice that had built around her heart melt, but casually said, "Fine. Okay, I am going to wait, but if you aren't here in the next fifteen minutes, I'm leaving."

Kevin agreed before hanging up. Kaandra stood next to the escalator and waited impatiently. Fifteen minutes passed before she finally saw him and could take inventory. Six feet tall, chocolate brown skin. Check. Receding hairline. She could work with that, especially with that handsome face. And he was a good dresser too. He wore dark brown pants and a fresh white shirt that perfectly highlighted his skin. His shoes were terrible, but she guessed you couldn't win them all. But what was with all the jewelry? She counted 1, 2…5 silver necklaces, a handful of rings, and bracelets. Who did he think he was, some kind of hustler?

Kaandra sighed. She'd come all this way, and he'd been so nice on the phone. Just because Mr. Right didn't pass her entire checklist didn't mean she shouldn't give him a chance.

Kevin smiled as he approached Kaandra. "I'm so glad you waited for me. Would you like some lunch?"

Kaandra relaxed a bit at his smile. "Sure, how about at Antonio's?" She figured she deserved a nice lunch after being kept waiting, and he seemed more than happy to oblige.

Kaandra sighed softly to herself and gave an affirmative nod to whatever Kevin just asked. She had a smile plastered on her face, but she'd lost track of what he was talking about a while ago. He wasn't a bad guy, but she was bored. Maybe he wasn't Mr. Right after all…

"What are they like?" Kevin asked, breaking through her trance.

"Hmm?" Kaandra asked, suddenly aware that he was looking at her intently, waiting for her response to a question she hadn't completely heard. "I'm sorry. What was that?" she continued, embarrassed that she had been caught drifting.

"You've mentioned your daughters before." Kevin gave little indication that he knew he'd been ignored. "Monique and Brianna, right? What are they like?"

"Oh! They are my life," Kaandra responded. She got caught up in talking about her children and the whole mood of the date changed. Kevin listened intently as she described the ins and outs of her life as a single mom. She was even more pleased when he discussed his own children, and she couldn't hide her delighted smile when he went out to his car to grab some recent school pictures of them to show her.

The hours passed on, and soon their little lunch date began to turn into an all-night event. *I misjudged him*, Kaandra thought. They left lunch holding hands and window shopped through the mall until they found a coffee shop. Then they sat and drank coffee and talked until it closed.

"Guess it is time to go home," Kevin said, as he walked her out to her car. "I really don't want to say goodnight."

"I don't want to either," Kaandra said shyly.

"It doesn't feel like we have spent almost seven hours together" Kaandra said regretfully knowing that the date had to end at some point.

Kevin smiled and grabbed her hand, placing a light kiss on the back of it. "Goodnight, Kaandra. There will be other nights. I'll call you."

After that, Kaandra and Kevin's whirlwind romance began. Each date was better than the last, and Kaandra realized that she was falling for him.

"We need to talk," Kevin said, moving from where he and Kaandra were cuddling on the couch to turn off the movie they were watching.

Kaandra could feel her heart race at his serious tone. The last three months had been so good. "What's wrong? Did I do something?"

"No, no, it's nothing like that," Kevin said, moving to sit beside her again and taking her hands into his own. "My roommate is moving, and since the divorce, I can't afford to pay for a place of my own. I'm going to have to move to Maryland, to live with my mother."

Maryland? Kaandra thought. They already had trouble lining up their schedules to see each other as is. How would their relationship hold up to the distance? "Move in here," she said impulsively.

"What?"

"Move in here. I mean, you are here so often. You might as well. And then you don't have to live with your mother."

Kevin and his mother, Maria, were already at the restaurant waiting when Kaandra got there. Kaandra was finally going to meet Kevin's mother. Kevin thought it was finally the right time for them to meet, since things had gotten so serious. She could see them through the lobby window, looking impatient. Kaandra took one last look in her visor mirror, patting a few hairs into place, before taking a deep breath and stepping out of the car.

When she walked in, Kevin turned, as if sensing her presence, and breathed a calming sigh. "There you are," Kevin said, tenderly. "We were beginning to worry."

"I'm so sorry for making you wait. Traffic was terrible," Kaandra said. Then she walked up to Maria and politely put out a hand. "It is so wonderful to meet you, Maria. Sorry to keep you waiting."

Maria returned her greeting with a quick, loose handshake, and then said, "Oh good, now we can finally eat."

Kevin gave Kaandra a slight smile and rolled his eyes behind his mother's back. Then the three of them went to the host to let them know their entire party had arrived. It seemed even the host had been waiting on Kaandra because he immediately led them to their table. The restaurant was a nice place, glistening white china shown on warmly colored tablecloths, a live band played in the corner, providing delicate accompaniment to the happy conversation of eating guests, and crystalline lights created an inviting atmosphere.

It was the nicest place Kaandra had been to in a long while, but Maria just sniffed disappointedly after the host sat them. "What's wrong, Mother?" Kevin asked.

"We are right under the air conditioning. I'm going to freeze all thru dinner," she replied.

Kevin flagged another host down and asked if they could be seated somewhere else, and the host happily obliged. Kaandra hadn't seen anything wrong with their previous table, but was delighted to see that they were being seated closer to the band. "Don't they sound so good?" she said as they all sat down.

Maria sucked her teeth, but sat as well. "If you like deafening guitars in your ear while you eat, but at least this table is warmer."

Kaandra ignored the comment and tried to focus on ordering her meal, as did everyone else. The waitress came and went. She was pleasant enough, considering how busy the place was, but Maria just kept on about how rude and slow the woman was and how she had looked at her funny when she took her order. On and on she went about how terrible it all was, but when it was time for the check and the waitress asked how everything was, Maria simply smiled sweetly and said, "It was wonderful, dear."

Kaandra quickly finished up her meal, waived for the waitress and asked for the bill. She wanted to get away from Maria and the uncomfortable situation as soon as possible and get back to her home. The waitress came quickly and Kevin paid the bill. Kaandra said goodnight to Maria and left Kevin and Maria in the restaurant's parking lot. Kevin was supposed to drop off his mother at her hotel and then head home. After the awkward meal, Kaandra was relieved to be away, but her relief was short-lived. Two hours later, Kevin came home with his mother in tow. "Mother wasn't comfortable staying at the hotel alone. I told her she could stay with us," Kevin explained.

Hoping to start fresh and get in her good graces, Kaandra agreed to the arrangement. She helped Kevin get his mother comfortable in their room, and she took the couch while Kevin slept nearby on the floor. During the night, Kaandra heard someone crying, so she got up to check on the girls. Her daughters were fast asleep, but light was coming out from under her bedroom door and she could hear Maria talking to someone. She started to check on her, but the tone of her voice made her uneasy. Thinking it best to leave her alone, Kaandra crept back to the living room to go back to sleep, but sleep was elusive.

The next morning Kaandra left for work, tired but grateful that the previous night was behind her. She just had to get through her work day and things would be back to normal, or so she thought. As if on cue, the sudden ringing of her cellphone dashed her thoughts. It was Kevin, so she hit the speakerphone button and asked, "Did I forget something? I'm almost at work."

"No," Kevin said, sounding hesitant, "I just needed to tell you something."

"Sure, what's up? Did your mom make her train okay?"

"About that...Mom didn't go home. She needs to stay with us for a few weeks."

"A few weeks? Kevin, I don't know. Our place isn't that big..."

"It's just a few weeks, Kaandra. I don't get to see my mother often, and she is getting older..." Kevin pleaded.

"Fine, I can tell it is important to you. She can stay," Kaandra agreed. What was a few weeks to keep him happy?

Kaandra walked through her front door exhausted after a sleepless night and hard day at work and a bit apprehensive about what she would find. To her surprise, however, she walked into a spotless home and delicious smells coming from the kitchen. Perhaps she had overreacted and Maria's stay wouldn't be all bad.

"Kevin, is that you?" Maria called from the kitchen.

"No, ma'am, it's me, Kaandra."

"Oh, welcome home, could you come to the kitchen when you have a moment. I want to know what you think of this dinner I'm making."

Kaandra slipped her heels off, set down her purse and keys, and walked towards the kitchen. Maria was bustling around the kitchen in a flowery apron that she must have brought with her. If Kaandra didn't know any better she might have thought Maria's stay was planned. Kaandra quickly brushed that thought aside and walked into the kitchen. Maria had several pots and pans going and they were bubbling on the stove. The whole kitchen was full with smells of garlic, onion, and other savory treats. Kaandra's stomach rumbled hungrily as she stood next to the stove.

"Well, come over here and have a taste. Don't be shy," Maria said with a smile. Kaandra went to grab a saucer so she could sample whatever Maria was cooking up, but she was stopped. "Oh, you don't need that. No need to dirty another dish. Come on over here, and hold out your hand." Kaandra did as she asked, and before she could react, Maria grabbed a spoonful of sauce from one of the pots and poured it directly into her palm. Kaandra yelped and ran over to the sink to wash off the scalding liquid. Behind her, she heard Maria tsk. "Oh dear, was that too hot?"

The next few weeks Maria did everything she could to torment Kaandra. When Kevin wasn't around, Maria criticized Kaandra's every move. She was making sure it was clear that Kaandra was not good enough for her son. If Kaandra complained, Maria would lie and say she had said no such thing and would even go out of her way to praise her. But Kaandra stuck it out for Kevin's sake. She chauffeured her around and simply smiled through the insults, until finally it was over. Two weeks passed and Maria announced that she was going home. Finally, Kaanda would have her home back. The nightmare was finally over...

Or so she thought. It was only a few days later that she received the first phone call. "I'm sure you're happy now that I'm gone," Maria said the moment the phone was answered. Kaandra was silent and startled. This was true, but saying so would just start a fight. "Well, what do you have to say? I'm sure you're already whispering your lies into my son's ear, you conniving bitch."

Stunned, Kaandra simply hung up, but the calls kept coming, and they got nastier and nastier. The final one started with Maria accusing Kaandra of stealing her apron. This was the first time Kaandra had heard about the missing apron.

"What are you even going to use it for? My son doesn't want your nasty cooking," Maria spat into the phone. No amount of explanation or conversation could calm her down. She was convinced that the theft had occurred.

Unable to take the tirade of accusations and insults any longer, Kaandra slammed the phone down and called Kevin. "You have to do something about your mother. You should hear the things she has called me and accused me of doing."

"Kaandra, calm down, I'm sure it is just a misunderstanding."

"A misunderstanding? Really, is it a misunderstanding to call me a bitch? You have to do something about her. I can't take this any longer."

"Fine, I'll call her, but I really don't think..."

Kaandra hung up the phone on Kevin. The sooner he got off the phone with her, the sooner he could call his mother. A while passed and the phone rang. She answered it, expecting Kevin, but instead heard Maria. She was screaming almost incoherently at first, but Kaandra could make out, "You lying bitch. You told my son I was harassing you?"

"Yes, I told him the truth," Kaandra answered coldly.

"I warned my son about you. You just want him all to yourself so you can use him. You are nothing but a gold diggin' ho."

Kaandra laughed a bit at that. "Right," she said sarcastically. Kevin didn't have any money. She was the one helping him because his divorce had left him almost penniless.

"Oh, you think that is funny? Well, how's this for funny. I don't want to ever see you again. You are not welcome in my home, with or without my son," Maria screamed into the phone. Then she hung up and it was over.

Kaandra was relieved. She'd no longer have to deal with that unstable tyrant. She hated to put Kevin in the middle, but something had had to be done about his mother. To imagine a mother could be so cruel.

Kaandra stared at the two lines in shock. This wasn't how things were supposed to be. Things were finally on track. She had a good man, yes, but she wasn't ready for this. *They* weren't ready for this. They had only been together a little over a year and now this pregnancy was definitely going to add pressure to their new relationship. Kaandra had promised herself that with her next child, if there was one, that she would do it right. She would be sure the man was the right one and they would be married. She couldn't believe this was happening, but each test said the same thing, and she had taken several. She was positively pregnant again.

She wasn't sure how to tell Kevin, so she left the test out in the open for him to find. All day long she was nervous. How would he react? Did he even want more children? Kids hadn't really been something they had discussed.

Eventually, she began to hope that this would be good news. Perhaps he'd find the test and be overjoyed at the unexpected surprise. Finally, he came home, and after greeting her, he went to the bathroom. Kaandra waited anxiously for him to get out, but when he did, he acted as if nothing was new. She couldn't believe he hadn't seen the test. She had left it out in plain sight for him to see, but time passed and he still acted as if he hadn't seen it. Maybe he had just completely overlooked it.

Nervously, Kaandra slipped into the bathroom and grabbed the test. She walked back out to Kevin, took a deep breath, and handed it to him. "I have something you need to see." Kevin stared at the test, but didn't say anything. Kaandra waited anxiously, trying to be patient and let him process the news, but when he still didn't say anything, she couldn't take it. "Well, I'm pregnant. What do you think?"

"I'll support you with whatever you decide," Kevin said quietly.

"Whatever I decide?" Kaandra began to ask before realizing what he meant. "Oh, I see." She had waited all day for this moment and it wasn't at all what she expected. She had longed for at least comfort from him that things would be okay, and if she was being honest with herself, she had even hoped that this would be happy news. But this did not sound like a man excited to be a father. "I'll call the doctor's office in the morning …."

"When was your last period?" the medical assistant asked while staring down at her tablet.

"What? Sorry," Kaandra responded. She had been distracted by her surroundings and thoughts of how Kevin reacted the week before. The fluorescent lighting seemed harsh and glaring, but it was a nice enough room. For a local clinic, they had tried to make it welcoming. There were even flowers, though fake, brightening up the otherwise white and stainless steel décor.

"Are you taking any medications?" the woman asked again, this time looking up over her tablet to smile understandingly at her. "Yes, I am taking Zoloft" Kaandra responded.

"Hmm…that could be a problem if you are pregnant. I will let the doctor know. She will be in soon.

It took a while before someone finally returned. Finally, a doctor walked in with the aforementioned tablet in hand. She smiled kindly as she walked in. "Hi, sorry to keep you waiting. It's Kaandra, right?"

"Yes, that is correct."

Based on the information you've given us, and the blood test, you are at least three months along"

"Three months, really?"

"Are you sure?" Kaandra asked.

"I am, the blood tests are pretty accurate. But you look like you could use a minute to digest this news" the doctor said kindly. Then she walked out to give her some time alone.

Kaandra couldn't believe this. She'd always believed things happened for a reason and that there were signs of what to do, if you only paid attention. Suddenly, Kaandra knew what she had to do.

Kaandra breathed a sigh of hope as she jumped down off the table. As she dressed, a smile began to creep across her face and her hand trailed down to her abdomen. Whatever came next, she was sure that having this baby was the right decision for her.

"Hello, Kaandra," the caller said the moment the phone was answered.

It had been a peaceful three months since she'd heard that voice, but the moment she heard it, she was annoyed. "What, Maria," Kaandra said.

"So, my son told me you are pregnant." There was no hint of pleasure in the woman's voice. None of the warmth one would expect from a grandmother.

"Yes, you are going to be a grandmother," Kaandra said, hoping the realization would soften her a bit.

"I'm already a grandmother. This is the last thing Kevin needs right now. Why didn't *you* use protection?"

Kaandra couldn't believe it. Was she truly putting all the blame on her? Like she was the only one that caused her to get pregnant. "Not that it is any of your business, but we did, and your son is just as responsible for this as I am. I didn't get pregnant by myself!"

"Sure. He also told me that you were going to get an abortion, but then didn't. He told me some ridiculous excuse about you being allergic to anesthesia." Maria sniffed in disgust and disbelief. "You are just doing this control my son and take his money. You planned this all…"

"Is that what your son told you?" Kaandra yelled. "I was never going to have an abortion; your son lied to you. You probably need to talk to him to find out why he feels he needs to lie to you."

Kaandra slammed the phone down angrily. She couldn't stand that woman and didn't want to listen to false accusations.

But then it dawned on her, like it or not, this woman was her baby's family. There was no getting rid of her.

"Mother's new place is great. She's getting it all set up the way she likes it," Kevin said as he walked in.

Kaandra tiredly climbed to her feet and walked over to greet him. It was late, but she had been determined to stay up to see him, first trimester tiredness be damned. "That's nice," she responded, trying to sound genuine.

"You should come up and see it now that she's moved in, especially since you spent all that time helping me clear up my credit so I could help mother buy the house."

"I was happy to help," Kaandra said, slipping her arms around Kevin's neck. "And I'm even happier you're home." She went to kiss him, but he pulled away in his excitement to tell her about his mother's home.

"It's so close to my job that I'll get to check in on her. Mother's pleased about that."

"I bet she is." Kaandra mumbled under her breathe.

"I might stay with her some nights when I work late," Kevin continued. "It isn't good for her to be alone all the time anyway."

They say that absence makes the heart grow fonder, but Kaandra was beginning to believe that absence leads to a lot of lonely nights that can get a girl thinking. One night, Kevin had called to tell her that he had to work late and was going to stay at his mother's that night. Kaandra had been relieved that he had a safe place to stay and she wouldn't have to worry about him falling asleep at the wheel. But one night turned to two, and then a week. A week turned to a month, until finally Kevin had told her that he was going to move in with his mother since it was so close to his job.

Kaandra had tried not to be disappointed. It had made sense, really. Kevin had only been staying with her because he needed a place to stay, and she had worried about him driving the long way after work each night. They had talked it out, and Kevin had told her he would come down on the weekends to see her. She was happy to not have to worry about him, and on the plus side, the change seemed to get his mother off her back, but she certainly missed him.

The worst were the weekends he didn't come home. Too often he'd call and explain that he couldn't come down for the weekend because of overtime, but one week he called and said he couldn't come down because his mother needed him to take her shopping. Kaandra had blown up on him.

"Shopping, you can't be serious?" she'd said sarcastically. "Why does she need you to drive her around?"

"She doesn't like driving in the busy traffic, and her eyes aren't that great. She shouldn't be driving anyway," Kevin had explained.

"But why this weekend? You weren't able to come down last weekend either. I miss you." Kaandra had felt tears well up in her eyes. Her pregnancy hormones were raging, but she wasn't sure her tears were solely caused by them.

"She needs me, Kaandra."

"I need you too!" she'd yelled. "This is exactly what your mother was hoping for …. She's trying to break us up."

Kevin had calmed her down, eventually soothing her fears and promising that he'd be down the next week. Nothing could stop him, he'd told her. He had kept his word, but there were other weekends missed due to work and there was still every night in between. The nights alone caused her to think about her relationship. In the dark, lonely moments, a voice inside her questioned whether or not Kevin was actually "Mr. Right." Was he dependable? Would he be around for her and her children? She wasn't so sure anymore.

Kaandra woke suddenly to the sound of her front door opening. She had been sleeping well, having finally gotten Kiara to sleep. Kiara was only 3 months old and would wake up every few hours for her feedings. So getting everyone in the bed to sleep early was a welcomed miracle. Especially, since she had a test in the morning. She'd been doing well in her classes, all A's this semester, but she couldn't afford to slack off. With two young children and a newborn that she was essentially raising on her own, she had too little time to study or sleep.

She'd enrolled in a Paralegal degree program while she was still pregnant with Kiara. She'd taken a semester off after Kiara was born, but now she was attending full time again. Her time was filled with work, her children, and school. The little sleep she got was precious and often rare, so her first thought at waking was one of annoyance.

Kaandra swiped a tired hand across her eyes and looked at the clock. It was after 2 a.m. What was going on? It then dawned on her that she was hearing noises in her home late at night. This woke her up quickly. She jumped to her feet and was on her way out the bedroom to grab her kids when her bedroom door opened.

Kaandra gasped in shock and fear, but quickly realized who it was. "Kevin, what are you doing here? I thought you said you couldn't come down this weekend."

Kevin looked frenzied and nervous as he stood in the doorway. He rubbed his hands together and seemed at a loss for what to say. "Oh, Kaandra, you're awake."

"Well, yes, I heard the door. It's late. You scared me. What are you doing here?"

"I just wanted to see you. I'm sorry I scared you. I couldn't wait." Kevin smiled and walked over to her. He grabbed her in a hug and pulled her close. "Aren't you happy to see me?"

Kaandra softened at his touch. Their time together was not nearly often enough. "Of course, I am." She leaned into his arms and kissed him softly. "You just startled me. I'm glad you are here though."

Kevin smiled and kissed her back. Then he suddenly got excited and moved away. "I really am sorry I scared you, but I'm here for a reason, and I just couldn't wait."

"What is it?"

"This," Kevin said, dropping to one knee before her. He reached into his pocket and pulled out a ring. "Will you marry me?"

Kaandra stood there in shock and put hand over her mouth. She had dreamed of Kevin proposing for a while now. This wasn't what she had expected, but it was happening all the same. As he knelt there before her, smiling, a bit of a plea in his eyes, she knew what her answer should be.

"Yes," Kaandra said. "Yes, of course, I will marry you." Kevin might not always be right, but he was her Mr. Right, and now they were finally going to be a family.

Six long months had gone by and Kaandra was going to finally get her dream wedding. "Tara, it's beautiful," Kaandra said, taking in the sight of the decorated reception hall. Her little sister and maid of honor, Tara, and her bridesmaids had made it look like a fairy tale. The aroma from the flowers filled the air and everything glistened and gleamed.

"So, you like it?" Tara asked, beaming proudly.

"Like it? I love it. It is beautiful. We never could have done this if you hadn't helped," Kaandra said. She grabbed her sister in a big hug and then pushed her back to look her in the eye. "I hope you didn't spend too much on all of this."

Tara waved her off. "Think nothing of it. I just want my big sis to have the wedding of her dreams. Just consider it your wedding present, besides..."

Kaandra never got to hear what else her sister was going to say because at that exact moment Kaandra's phone rang. "Sorry, it's Kevin. Just a moment... Hello? Kevin? What? What's wrong?" After a heated discussion, Kaandra hung up. "I can't believe it! I knew she would something dramatic. She just wants to ruin our wedding."

"What's wrong?" Tara asked.

"That mother of his is refusing to come." Kaandra fumed. "He drove all the way out there to get her and now she is saying that she isn't coming. He's pleading with her right now to come. He's going to be late for his own rehearsal and dinner."

"Kaandra, breathe," Tara said. Then she took her phone. "Give your phone to me. I'll take care of any calls you get. You go and enjoy your rehearsal dinner. This is your night. Let me take care of the problems."

This was it, her wedding day, finally. After the stress of the rehearsal last night and the frenzy of this morning, she was honestly ready to just get on with it. Kaandra had been a mess the night before and was still feeling spent from the ordeal. Because of his mother's tantrum, Kevin had been late arriving to the rehearsal, which had caused some harsh words between the two of them. Then the best man hadn't been able to make it because of some sort of car trouble. Everything had seemed doomed from the start, but Tara had kept everything running as smoothly as possible, so most of the guests were none the wiser, but it had still made Kaandra feel some type of way. Without her sister there, she wasn't sure what she would have done. Kaandra looked over where her sister was standing, talking to someone on the phone, and smiled.

But when her sister hung up and turned around, Kaandra could feel the smile fading from her face. It was a look she had come to know well over the last couple of days. She had bad news, but was trying to stay calm. "What is going on, Tara? I know that look," Kaandra asked.

"Kaandra, I want you to stay calm. I have already figured everything out, and it is all going to be fine," Tara told her, plastering a smile on her face that hadn't quite reached her eyes.

"Okay..."

"The photographer is running late—"

"What? We can't start without the photographer. Everything is ru—"

"Kaandra, it will be okay," Tara said calmly and grasped her sister by the shoulders. "We are just going to rearrange things. We'll take group photos after the wedding ceremony. They will be just as beautiful, before or after. We'll just let everyone know that we'll be a little late to the reception. The hall is already open, so people can go ahead and go in. It will be fine."

Kaandra took a deep breath and nodded. "Yes, you are right. That will work. Thank you, Ta—"

Just then, a gentleman in a suit and tie came in. Kaandra didn't recognize him as one of the wedding guests. Perhaps someone from Kevin's side? "Um, Kaandra?" the man asked, looking nervous.

"Yes?"

"Um, well, I'm the limo driver for your mother-in-law."

"Oh, yes, hi. What's wrong?" Kaandra asked. She looked up at the clock on the wall in her dressing room. "You should have already been there to pick her up. Did you have trouble finding the address?"

"No ma'am, I found it. It's just, "the man started nervously before pausing. Finally, he continued, "I waited for her, and when she didn't come out, I knocked on her door. Well, she finally answered, but she is refusing to come."

"Of course she is." Kaandra fumed for a moment, and then the tears started to come.

Tara immediately stepped in and grabbed Kaandra in a hug. Over her shoulder, she told the driver thank you for his service and that he could go. "Shh, shh, it's okay, calm down."

"That crazy woman, I knew she'd do something like this. She promised Kevin last night that she would be here. She'd made some ridiculous excuse about not having a dress, and that is why she wouldn't come last night, but this is really about me. She doesn't like me, so she is trying to ruin our wedding by not coming." Kaandra continued to cry, but her tone had more anger than sadness in it.

Tara held her until the tears stopped, and then said, "This isn't about her. This is about you and Kevin. You are the ones getting married. If she doesn't want to be here, then good riddance." Tara hugged her and then grabbed her hand. "Come on, let's fix your makeup. You've got a wedding to get to."

Kaandra felt like a princess. There had been some bumps along the way, but the ceremony had been lovely, and she was finally married to Kevin. Now, as she twirled around with her husband, she felt like all the worries were being swept away. Nothing could dash her happiness in this moment, not schedule changes or Maria's refusal to come. She was married now. She had wondered a few times whether they would ever end up here, but as she looked up into his handsome face, all those worries were gone. Well, mostly.

The song ended and the DJ announced, "Let's give a round of applause to our happy couple." The guests clapped, breaking the spell, and Kaandra reluctantly let go of her husband. "And now I'd like to invite the mother of the groom to the dance floor for the traditional mother and son dance."

Kaandra stiffened. She had forgotten to cancel the dance after finding out that Maria refused to come. She waved her hand at the DJ to get his attention, but right as she started to say something, she was interrupted by polite clapping from the wedding guests. Maria had shown up after all.

Maria glided onto the dance floor and up to her son. She was all smiles, practically giddy, as Kevin grabbed her hands and pulled her along the floor. Kaandra was furious. She couldn't believe it, after all of the heartache and trouble, Maria had decided to show up to the reception. She had the nerve to smile and laugh like nothing was wrong. In fact, she looked like this was one of the happiest moments of her life.

It was then that Kaandra realized that married or not, Maria would always be around. Maria had certainly become a thorn in her side.

"How lovely," Kaandra said with excitement as she walked into the hotel lobby and up to counter. The plane ride to Myrtle Beach hadn't been long, but she'd still fallen into a deep sleep, exhausted from their wedding, so now she was energized and ready for the week of honeymooning they had ahead of them. "Isn't this beautiful, Kevin?"

"Hmm?" Kevin looked up from his phone distractedly. He looked around the hotel lobby as if he hadn't even noticed he had walked in.

"Feeling a little jet lag?" Kaandra asked. She walked over and squeezed him in a tight hug. "I said, 'Isn't this beautiful?'"

Kevin smiled and hugged her back with one arm, placing his phone back in his pocket as he did so. "I'm fine, just a little tired, I guess. I couldn't sleep like you," he added playfully. "But yes, it is very beautiful, like you." Kevin kissed her lightly on the cheek and then whispered in her ear, "We should check in."

Kaandra blushed slightly and walked up to the counter. "I'm here to check in," she told the front desk clerk.

"Of course, ma'am," the clerk responded. "What name are you checking in under?"

"Mr. and Mrs. Right," Kaandra happily answered, pleased to officially be able to call herself Mrs. Right.

Kaandra gave their bags to the bellhop to bring up, finished checking in, and walked to the elevator. She hit the button up and the doors opened as if waiting for them. Kaandra walked in, but suddenly Kevin reached into his pocket like he was looking for something and stepped off the elevator. "Shoot, I left something in the car. You go on ahead. I'll be right there. Room 313, right?"

"Yes, but can't it wait?" Kaandra asked, but the doors were already closing. She hit the button for the third floor. She was anxious to see the room they were staying in for the week. She just wished she was seeing it for the first time with him. It was silly, but she'd hoped he'd do something special, like whisk her off her feet and carry her across the threshold. She sighed. It wasn't like he planned on forgetting something. He'd be along soon enough.

"Shit, I forgot my wallet," Kevin said, patting his pockets and looking around as if he'd find the missing item on the ground.

"Don't worry about it," Kaandra said, already digging into her purse. "I'm sure it is just in the car or back at the hotel room. I'll pay for the tickets."

"No, no," Kevin said, sounding a bit frantic. "I'm sure I put it in my pocket. I must have dropped it. I better go back to the car and check."

He was already walking off before Kaandra could stop him. They'd been waiting in line to catch a movie, and the people in front of them had just finished up. The attendant looked at her expectantly and waved her forward. Embarrassed, Kaandra smiled at the attendant and stepped out of line. "Sorry, I guess we'll catch a later show."

Kaandra stood on the sidewalk, unsure of what to do with herself. Kevin had been preoccupied all day, ever since that call from his mother. She'd been calling every day since they'd left. The day before, while they were trying to get in a little sightseeing, he had gotten a call that upset him. She wasn't sure what was going on, but she could tell it was taking a toll on him. He didn't seem to want to talk about it though, so she left it alone. Honestly, she was just glad that she didn't have to deal with his mother.

Kaandra perused the shop windows near the theatre while she waited for Kevin to return. It took a while, but finally she saw him hurrying towards her. He looked happier, not nearly as concerned and distracted as he'd been before. "Did you find your wallet?" she asked when he got closer.

"What?" he asked.

"Your wallet?"

"Oh, yes, yes I did," he said, fishing into his pocket to pull it out. "Sorry, didn't hear you at first. Ready to see that movie?" he continued all in one breath.

Kaandra followed him back to the box office queue, but she couldn't shake the nagging feeling that something had changed. Kevin seemed relaxed, perky almost, not distracted and concerned like he had been. *Stop it, Kaandra*, she thought. *Are you really wishing he was upset? It is a good thing that he is happy.* But Kaandra still wondered what had happened during his walk to the car.

Kaandra frowned as she watched her husband walk out the door. "Back to reality" she hummed. They'd had an amazing honeymoon week but now they were back to everyday life, which meant Kevin had to go back to work. Once again, he was leaving her and wouldn't be back until the weekend. That aspect of their relationship hadn't changed. He'd been traveling from Virginia to Washington D. C for work for a couple years and staying with his mother during the week. She knew the travel put stress on him and on their relationship. Something had to be done.

Well, it's about time to move, I guess, Kaandra thought. She sat down at the computer and started to look for places to live in Washington D. C. *I'm his wife. If he can't come here, I'll go to him.*

Home, sweet home, Kaandra thought as she parked the U-Haul outside the apartment complex they would be living in. After only four months of searching Kevin had found an apartment that would fit all of them, was within budget and was close to his job. Finally, they were going to be a family, all living in one place. She honked the horn to let Kevin know she had arrived and hopped happily out of the cab of the truck. The kids were staying with her parents so that they wouldn't be in the way while moving.

Kaandra saw Kevin and ran over to him. "Happy New Year!" she shouted before giving him kiss.

Kevin laughed. "It's the 2nd, baby."

"Well, yes, but I didn't get to ring in the New Year with you, and this is a new start for us. It counts." She wrapped her arms around his neck and pulled him into another kiss, this time showing him how much she'd missed him.

"Oh good, you've made it."

Kaandra stiffened at the sound of Maria's voice and pulled away from Kevin. "Oh, Maria," she said, trying to keep any disdain from her voice. "You didn't tell me your mother would be coming, Kevin. Is she here to help us move in?" Kaandra didn't think that Maria should be lifting boxes, nor did she think she'd offer to help anyway, unless it was to criticize with how she wanted to decorate.

"Oh, didn't I tell you? She lives just a street over," Kevin answered, beaming. "I forgot you hadn't actually visited her before. She was just here to keep me company until you got here."

"Oh, that's nice."

"Isn't it? She'll be able to help with the kids when we both have to work."

Kaandra just smiled and nodded. How could she have not realized that they would be so close to her mother-in-law? Home, sweet home, indeed.

Kaandra leaned back in her chair and stretched her back from where she'd been bent over her computer keyboard. She'd been working as a paralegal at a law firm for a few months now. Kaandra was excited to finally be using her degree that she worked so hard to get. She didn't think she would make it through the final semester because she had a newborn but her hard work and perseverance had paid off. She loved the job and had even been able to make some new friends, Susan and Pedro, which was nice to have in a town so far from home. The days sitting at a desk could start to take a strain on her back and staring at the computer screen made her eyes tired.

She was rubbing her eyes with the palms of her hands when her cellphone rang. It was her oldest daughter, Monique. "Hi, sweetie," Kaandra answered. "I'm not supposed to be on my phone at work. Is something wrong?"

"I'm sorry, Mommy," Monique answered, sounding upset. "I forgot my key and now we can't get in the house."

"Did you try knocking really loud on the door so Kevin could let you in?" Kaandra asked. The key was only supposed to be a precaution. Kevin was supposed to be home with the baby. He had switched around his schedule so he could be home during the day while Kaandra was at work.

"I tried. We knocked really loudly, but he didn't answer." Monique sounded on the verge of tears. "I don't see his car either."

Kaandra tried to stay calm for her daughter's benefit. "Okay, I want you and Brianna to sit right there in front of the door. I will call your stepdad and see where he is. Don't go anywhere. I will call you back as soon as I finish calling him."

"Okay, Mommy."

Kaandra hung up the phone and quickly called Kevin. While listening to the rings, her mind spun with questions. Where was Kevin? Had something happened with Kiara? If so, why hadn't he called her to let her know? *Come on, pick up, Kevin*, she thought as the phone just continued to ring.

Finally, right before the voicemail would have picked up, Kevin answered. "Hello?" he said quietly.

"Kevin? Where are you?"

"Kaandra? What's wrong?" Kevin was speaking so quietly Kaandra could barely hear him, and he seemed annoyed.

"Why are you speaking so softly? I can barely hear you. And why aren't you home? Monique forgot her key and can't get inside, but she shouldn't even have to use it. You were supposed to be home. Is something wrong with, Kiara?" Kaandra was nearly in a panic now.

"What? No," Kevin answered, stumbling over his words. "No, it's nothing like that. I got called into work. An emergency meeting. Kiara is with my mother."

"Emergency meeting? Won't you be there later tonight? What am I supposed to do about Monique? I haven't been here long. I hate to ask to leave."

"Calm down, it will be okay. I'll call Mother, and she can let them in. I gave her a key a while back."

Kaandra grimaced at the idea that Maria had a key to their house, but she was grateful that someone would be able to help out. She hung up with Kevin and called Monique to tell her not to worry and that Maria would be over in a moment to let her in. Everything was going to be okay. But after hanging up, Kaandra couldn't help but go over her conversation with

Kevin repeatedly in her mind. She'd never known for Kevin to be called in to an emergency meeting, and his tone had seemed off. She just couldn't shake the nagging feeling that something was wrong.

"I already told you, I got held over at work!" Kevin yelled.

"All night, Kevin?" Kaandra said as she gathered up her things. "And you couldn't call me? Or answer your phone when I called you? I was worried sick about you."

"I came home as soon as I could. You know how crazy things have been lately."

"You conveniently got home just in time for me to go to work," Kaandra said. It all just seemed a little too neat to her at the moment. "I already don't see you enough as is, with all these trips you've been going on for work, and now you can't even come home when you say you will?"

"Kaandra, I'm sorry. I already explained that my phone died."

"And you couldn't borrow another phone? Are you telling me your whole building doesn't have a phone you could use?"

"It got late. I didn't want to wake you."

"Whatever," Kaandra said, interrupting his excuses. She grabbed her keys and walked to the door. "I can't be late to work. We will talk about this later." As she walked out the door, Kaandra was heated. Tears were forming at the corners of her eyes. She knew this wasn't right, but she didn't want to think about what it could mean.

Kaandra was trying to put aside the events of that morning and focus on work, but it was proving to be difficult. She was grateful when it was finally time for her lunch break so that she could relax for few minutes. But just as she was sitting down to eat, she got a phone call. It was from a number she didn't recognize, so she almost ignored it. Something told her to answer it though.

"Who is this?" the woman calling asked as soon as Kaandra answered.

"Who is this?" Kaandra asked back with an attitude. "You called me."

"This number keeps showing up on my boyfriend's cellphone. Who are you?"

"Who's your boyfriend?" As if somehow knowing what the woman would say, Kaandra didn't want to ask, but she had to know.

"Kevin Right."

Kaandra felt the room spin. Her heart raced. Tears leapt to her eyes and at the same time her ears rang with anger. "Kevin Right? Is that what you said?"

"Yes, now who is this?"

"I'm his wife, Mrs. Right."

"His wife?" The woman on the other end of the line sounded just as shocked as Kaandra felt. Both women sat on the phone in silence as the minutes ticked by, both unsure what to do with this realization of betrayal.

Finally, one of them decided they needed to talk, and talk they did. It all seemed to make sense to Kaandra. The late nights, the emergency meetings, even Kevin's frenzied proposal now made sense. Hell, it was even possible that Maria's attitude was caused by all of this. He'd been playing her for months, or years, perhaps entire three years she'd known him. Who knew? She certainly didn't know who Mr. Right was anymore.

She'd come home early from work with a coldness in her heart after talking to Kevin's mistress.

The moment she'd walked through the door, she heard herself ask, "Have you been cheating on me?" Just like that, no tears, no anger. Just a question that she already knew the answer too. The kids were at Maria's. Whether it was because Kevin sensed there would be a fight or because he was planning on sneaking out with his mistress, Kaandra never found out, and she really didn't care.

"Of course not, Kaandra. I told you it was work. You're just being paranoid," Kevin had said.

It was the "paranoid" that set her off. All this time she'd been made a fool of. Every time she questioned him about his whereabouts or told him the way his mother treated her, he'd acted like something was wrong with her. He'd made her feel crazy at even thinking something could be wrong. But she'd been right all along.

Kaandra flew into a rage. All the pain came bursting out at once. "Paranoid? Really? Is this paranoid?" At that point, she called his mistress back, putting her on speaker phone. "Trinity, Kevin says that I'm being paranoid. He says he's never cheated on me. What do you have to say about all of that?"

The rest of the day seemed like a bad dream. She remembered his shock when he'd first heard the other woman's voice and then how he'd tried to say he didn't know her. That it was a mistake. That she was just trying to cause trouble.

Kaandra knew she'd yelled at him and at one point tried to slap him and must have blacked out. When she awoke from the blackout she saw her hand was bruised and the cops coming thru her front door. The cops must have been called by some neighbors, but Kaandra could not immediately recall the events that just happened…the cops asked her some questions and said one of them had to leave. And just like that it was over. She'd packed a bag and walked out the door.

The next few days were hazy. Tara, once again had been a lifesaver, volunteering to pick-up her nieces so they could to stay with her. She couldn't take away Kaandra's pain, but she'd done all she could for her, by giving her some much needed time on her own to figure things out. The break gave her a chance to clear her mind and begin divorce proceedings.

Susan, her friend from work, offered to let her stay with her family. At first she'd refused, but the five long nights in the hotel only depressed her further, so eventually she accepted. The night she went to stay with them she'd nearly broken down. She couldn't believe that this was where her life had ended up. Once again, she'd been heartbroken. She'd looked for "Mr. Right" and gotten a counterfeit. She didn't know where to go from here.

But Susan's family welcomed her like one of their own. They didn't let her wallow in her grief. She ate at the dinner table with them, joined in their conversations, and even in their family activities. For that, Kaandra was eternally grateful.

It had been a three long weeks since Kaandra had confronted Kevin, which had changed her life forever. She thought long and hard about what she should do next. Eventually, Kaandra put in her resignation at work. She loved her job, but she wanted to be back home with her family. Though she'd only been there a short while, her coworkers were sad to see her go. Her boss even went out of her way to help her find a new position back home. On her last day, they threw her a big going away party. It was then that she realized that she was leaving behind a lot of good as well as bad. She'd been hurt, but even in the midst of her pain, there were those who were kind and valued her. That had to mean something.

"Welcome home, girls," Kaandra said, unlocking the door while balancing Kiara on her hip. Monique and Brianna giggled and laughed as they ran into the small apartment, taking in the old and new furniture and decorations as they did so. Kaandra had been working on the apartment for a couple weeks to get it all settled before the kids moved in. She wanted it to feel like home from their first day there. They'd been through enough chaos lately. Kaandra was grateful that she and the girls had been able to stay with family until their new place was ready.

"Which one is our room?" Monique called out.

"The one with the pink walls," Kaandra answered, smiling at their delight. Kiara babbled happily, picking up on their excitement. "And welcome home to you too," she said, squeezing her tightly. "Do you like our new home?"

A knock on the door interrupted her, and she walked over to see who it could be. She'd met a few of her neighbors while getting the apartment ready and several of them had kids who wanted to meet the girls. Maybe they'd noticed they'd move in. But when Kaandra answered the door, it wasn't a neighbor. It was the mailman.

"Mrs. Right?" the man asked.

Kaandra cringed at her soon to be changed name, but answered, "Yes, that's me."

"I have a certified letter for you," he said and pulled out a green card. "Please sign here."

Kaandra did as he asked and was handed an official looking envelope. As she held it, tears formed in her eyes. She knew what this was. With shaking hands, she opened it up and pulled out the stack of papers, her divorce papers. It was done. Mr. and Mrs. Right were no more.

As she stood in the open doorway holding the final chapter of her marriage to Mr. Right, Kaandra could hear her daughters laughing and playing in their room. Kiara was rambling in baby talk that was already spattered with actual words. The sounds were joyful, and Kaandra suddenly felt at peace. She hadn't felt that in months. She stood still a moment to savor the feeling. She knew she still had battles to deal with, but today she was going to linger in the newfound feeling. She'd get through this like she had every other problem. Everything would be alright.

"Let's go see what your sisters are up to, Kiara," Kaandra said. Then she closed the door behind her.

Made in the USA
Middletown, DE
02 December 2020